For my sons Jo and Leo
with whom 'Storytime' began

First published 1986 by
Walker Books Ltd
184-192 Drummond Street
London NW1 3HP

First printed 1986
Printed and bound by
L.E.G.O., Vicenza, Italy

British Library Cataloguing in Publication Data
Daly, Niki
Look at me!—(Storytime; 6)
I. Title   II. Series
823'.914[J]   PZ7

ISBN 0-7445-0272-1

LOOK AT ME!

Niki Daly

WALKER BOOKS
LONDON

When Andy came to play Suzie said,
'Let's play goodies and baddies.'

'OK,' said Andy. 'I'll be a goodie and you can be a baddie.'
'And I'll be the goodies' robot,' said Josh.

Josh put a cardboard box over his head.
'Hey, look! I'm a robot,' he shouted.

But Suzie was busy dressing Andy
in Josh's sheriff's outfit.

'I can make power come out of
my finger,' said Josh. 'Look at me!'

But Suzie didn't look. She was
too busy being a baddie.

Then Andy and Suzie played Super Heroes.
Josh sat in his box while the Super Heroes
battled with each other.

And then he thought of something.
'Look at me!' shrieked Josh. 'I'm
the Karate King!'
But the Super Heroes didn't have
time to look.

Josh ran after them. He climbed onto
a table and balanced
on one foot.
'Look at me,' he said softly.

But Andy and Suzie were looking at books.

'Shush!' Andy scowled. 'I'm reading!'

He had Josh's favourite book.

Suzie didn't even glance up.

Josh felt very cross. He put
his jacket over his head and
pulled an ugly face at Andy.

'Hey, look at Josh!' Andy said.

'He's a gorilla,' said Suzie.

'Can we be gorillas too?' asked Andy.

'Ug, ug,' said the gorilla.

So Andy and Suzie pulled their jumpers over their heads and they all acted like gorillas.

'Hey, look at me!' called Josh.
They looked.
Josh was smiling at them from
between his legs.

'You crazy gorilla,' laughed
Suzie. And she gave her
brother a big gorilla hug.